Shtetl Tales

Volume Seven

Eleanore Smith

authorHOUSE®

AuthorHouse™
1663 Liberty Drive
Bloomington, IN 47403
www.authorhouse.com
Phone: 833-262-8899

Published by AuthorHouse 03/16/2023

ISBN: 979-8-8230-0408-4 (sc)
ISBN: 979-8-8230-0407-7 (e)

Print information available on the last page.

Any people depicted in stock imagery provided by Getty Images are models, and such images are being used for illustrative purposes only. Certain stock imagery © Getty Images.

This book is printed on acid-free paper.

Because of the dynamic nature of the Internet, any web addresses or links contained in this book may have changed since publication and may no longer be valid. The views expressed in this work are solely those of the author and do not necessarily reflect the views of the publisher, and the publisher hereby disclaims any responsibility for them.

Contents

PART TWO

Acknowledgements

I wish to dedicate this collection to the memory of my parents (Bertha and Philip Kastel), to the memory of Dr. Sumner Smith, to Len Paris, my editor, to my children (Karen, David and Heidi) and their spouses, to my grandchildren and their spouses, and to my great grandchildren.

Part One

Moishe Retires

Deep in their hearts the people of the little shtetl of Patchentuch always understood that one day their beloved Mayor of many years, Moishe Kapoyer, would retire for the final time, and one day he did. Contingency plans for his replacement were in order. These plans had established, with Moishe's approval, that his son, Chaim, would replace him as the Mayor of the town, and, hopefully, the world would not come to an end, which of course it did not.

Accordingly, when Moishe officially resigned for the fourth and final time, Chaim was formally sworn in to office, his first task being the selection of a new Council. This was an extremely daunting challenge to be sure, especially in Patchentuch where everyone always had a different opinion about everything, which they were more than willing to share. In this regard there had recently been a great deal of discussion in the community regarding the makeup of the new Council. According to some, especially many of the yentas, the existing Council had become just a gathering of intractable and dithering old men who were mired in tradition and bound to the old ways of doing things. Granted, these folks possessed the benefit of age and experience, but there was a hesitation, even a reluctance on their part to embrace any change and to move forward with the times, especially where the rights of women were concerned. Some on the Council had even opposed puppet shows because of the Biblical injunction against graven images. These were people who clung to the old ways like barnacles to a rock, and who were vehemently opposed to innovation. A new generation, however, had grown up in Patchentuch; these were, for example, those who left for America or who ran off to join the circus and walk the high wire. These young people were not afraid of change. They welcomed it. They were the bold and the brave. Some even championed the rights of women and dared to defy the narrow world of their parents. The flying Farshimmelts, for example, did not fear the outside world. They wanted desperately to be a part of it, but according to the fathers they were the Jews who might change their names and forget Patchentuch, altogether.

In any case, and in this environment of varied views, a new Council of six members was selected by The Honorable Mayor Chaim Kapoyer, son of the now legendary Moishe. Three of the new members were Pinchas Plotz, Beymish Schmootz and Yossel Fartumelt, all of whom were fairly traditional in their respective philosophies and life view. The other three members selected were Tevya Helfen, Gimmel Lochinkopf and Gideon Koach, all considered by most to be relatively progressive in thought and action.

The result was that because Mayor Chaim Kapoyer would have the deciding vote in case of a tie, and because Chaim, himself, mostly embraced the long held beliefs of his father, and the Jewish people, were a people of tradition, not much was expected to change in the little shtetl of Patchentuch, at least for the time being.

The Mitzvah

Rebbe Benny Rachmanes of Patchentuch received word that a new Rebbe for the neighboring town of Schmertzburg had been installed to replace their recently retired Rebbe. Upon hearing the news Rebbe Benny decided to pay a courtesy call to personally introduce himself and to welcome the new Rebbe, Dovid Plotznick. In general, relations between the people of both towns were cordial. There was one notable exception, however, and that was Geshmak Feinkochen of Patchentuch. In Geshmak's mind a serious competition existed between Patchentuch and Schmertzburg, a town that he considered substantially inferior to his own. True, Schmertzburg did not have a Mayor, a bank, a library or a lawyer, but they had managed quite well somehow without any of the above. At one time they had had a boat which had since been converted into a bathtub by the schnorrer, Pinchas Dumkopf, who had needed it more than anyone had needed a boat. In the mind of Geshmak Feinkochen mind, however, the very fact that Schmertzburg had once *had* a boat meant that they had *had* a navy, and most of his attention and all of his energies continued to be focused on any possible advantage Schmertzburg might gain in the future. Such a thing would never be allowed to happen if Geshmak had any say in the matter.

The meeting between Rebbe Benny and Rebbe Dovid Plotznick was pleasant and warm, and both men immediately took a liking to one another. Upon his return to Patchentuch Rebbe Benny made a report to the Council regarding his visit. He had returned with feelings of charity in his heart, and so he offered suggestions to the Town Council in this regard.

"It has occurred to me," Rebbe Benny stated, "that where we here in Patchentuch have been blessed with so much in regard to others, and in the interests of friendship, charity and neighborliness, we in our town have an obligation to demonstrate our gratitude by doing something good for our neighbors.

"Gratitude for what in particular?" exclaimed Pinchas Plotz. Pinchas, by the way, who had been a playful and good natured young chap, had become somewhat dour and heavy handed in his adult years, certainly not as light hearted as he once had been.

"Gratitude for all that we have," responded Rebbe Benny.

"And Schmertzburg is suffering?" asked Gimmel Lochinkopf.

"No, they are not suffering," replied Rebbe Benny, "but they lack many of the advantages that we in our town enjoy."

"Such as what?" persisted Pinchas.

"Such as, for example, a library, a bank, a puppet theatre, three lawyers and a Mayor."

"If they want a Mayor," added Beymish Schmootz, "they are free to elect one. If they want a library and a puppet theatre, what is stopping them?" At that point, and before the discussion became any more heated, which it seemed to be becoming, Gideon Koach stepped in.

"Have you ever heard of charity?" he asked.

"Why do they need charity?" asked Yossel Fartumel, as the Mayor listened patiently to the arguments offered by both sides of his divided Council.

"They don't *need* charity nor do they seek it," offered Tevya Helfen, and at that point the Mayor stepped in, thereby ending the debate, and he asked Rebbe Benny what he would suggest.

"I would suggest," the Rebbe responded, "that in my Shabbos sermon, with your approval, of course, I raise the subject of Mitzvah, and doing good in general, and how in neighborly celebration of Schmertzburg's new Rebbe, we in our town do something to mark the occasion. We are, after all, neighbors."

"And what would you suggest we do?" the Mayor asked.

"I think it would be appropriate," Rebbe Benny told the group, "that in the spirit of generosity we might help them to establish a library in their town, something they have never had."

"A library?" asked Pinchas Plotz.

"Yes, a library," the Rebbe responded. "Who can deny that access to books and to literature of all kinds is always a good thing," and so that is exactly what they did. The Mayor banged his gavel signifying the end of the debate and adoption of the Rebbe's proposal.

Eventually, with book contributions and the support of Patchentuch residents, and much to the extreme annoyance of Geshmak Feinkochen, "The Schmertzburg Branch of the Patchentuch Library," (as Geshmak would always call it) was established. Geshmak would continue to fulminate and bloviate, while most of the residents of the little town of Patchentuch continued to take pride in the generous Mitzvah they had performed for their neighbors.

Chaim Learns

In Mayor Chaim Kapoyer's opinion his councillors had not accorded Rebbe Benny the respect he was due when he had voluntarily appeared before the Council. The Rebbe had demonstrated a courtesy when presenting his ideas regarding the doing of a mitzvah in honor of the installation of the new Rebbe of Schmertzburg, when he could just as easily have gone over the heads of the Town Council with his mitzvah proposal. Instead, he had had the courtesy to present those ideas before the Council first, and, in turn, the Council had treated him rather poorly. After all, he *was* their Rebbe.

Mayor Chaim believed that he, himself, was largely responsible for the incident because he had not adequately controlled the meeting as he should have. He had not sufficiently asserted his authority as Mayor in order to deter the acrimonious debate that ensued. His father, Moishe, the previous Mayor would have done a far better job at maintaining respectful order, he believed. When he later related the unfortunate episode describing how Rebbe Benny had not received his due respect at the meeting, and how he, Chaim, had not succeeded in maintaining order, his wife, Tovah, was sympathetic.

"Oy, Chaim," she told him, "you are too hard on yourself. I am certain it was not that bad," but it was. It was then, however, that Tovah realized that her husband, if he was to become a successful Mayor, would need to become more assertive. He would seriously require assertiveness training.

A few days later a concerned Tovah, her mother Shayna and her daughter Leah had a discussion in the market place where they were shopping. Tovah explained the situation to her mother and daughter regarding the disastrous Council meeting which Chaim, in his own view, had not been able to control. The result had been an unexpected and uncomfortable experience for Rebbe Benny, who was, according to Chaim, not treated with due respect.

"Oy," Shayna told her daughter and granddaughter, "this cannot be not good."

"No," Tovah agreed, "it is not," and so it was decided that Chaim would need lessons, practice sessions, even, in learning to become assertive. The women would teach him, and it was decided that the three of them would give Chaim a crash course, which they subsequently did.

With Chaim's acquiescence they met together with his mother in law, his wife and daughter who all proceeded to give him the assertiveness instruction he required. Women innately understood such things, and sometimes even better than men, and so they went to work. They coached the Mayor, they encouraged him, and they iterated and reiterated in order to force the conception of assertiveness upon Chaim's reluctant mind. They even role played; that was the only way.

"Yes, Chaim, and now say it again with more conviction this time," his mother in law told him.

"Again, Chaim, say it again and louder," his wife instructed.

"No, father, you are still speaking too softly and tentatively," his daughter told him, and eventually after many practice sessions, Chaim began to get the hang of it, even began to enjoy it. Most of his adult life had been spent sharpening tools and knives in the family shop, not presiding over Council meetings as had his father when he was His Excellency. It would require time and practice, but with the help and support of his loyal cadre of three, his wife, his mother in law and his daughter, it would happen, and it eventually did. In time, the good people of the town came to trust and respect their new Mayor, The Honorable Chaim Kapoyer, who could be as assertive as necessary, when required. In fact, that is just what unruly and uncontrollable Counselors often needed and expected from their leader, and that is what the now esteemed Mayor of Patchentuch had become.

Good Will In Patchentuch

Despite the bloviations of Geshmak Feinkochen regarding his continuing obsession with besting his neighbors in Schmertzburg, the good will of the people of Patchentuch prevailed. Moreover, in his weekly sermon Rebbe Benny Rachmanes had presented a convincing and impassioned case espousing generosity to one's neighbors. In this regard, in addition to helping to establish The Schmertzburg Branch Of The Patchentuch Library, one of Patchentuch's citizens, Nasich Liebeherz, son of Melech Liebeherz, had another idea. Why not open a branch of their family Judaica Shop in Schmertzburg?

To this end Melech and Nasich visited the town, introduced themselves to the newly installed Rebbe Plotsky, and personally welcomed him. Since Schmertzburg had no Mayor they submitted their idea to Rebbe Plotsky, who thought the notion of a Judaica branch in his town to be inspired. Schmertzburg did not have such a shop, and so the concept was received with interest and much enthusiasm. After several trips to the town a small space was located in the Market Square, and arrangements were made to transfer inventory to the new Schmertzburg location. An assortment of kiddush cups, candlesticks and spice boxes was subsequently delivered to the new shop, and soon afterward, it opened for business.

As a result of the branch opening, the inventory in the Patchentuch shop had run low, so when Geshmak Feinkochen, of all people, came into the shop to purchase a replacement for the kiddush cup he had just gifted to his son and family, not much of a selection was available at the moment.

"So, this is what you have to show me?" he complained.

"For now, yes," Melech told him.

"So where is the selection you always have?" Geshmak persisted.

"At the Schmertzburg Branch," Melech told him, and that was all Geshmak needed to hear before exploding. It was not, according to him, bad enough that Schmertzburg all of a sudden had a Judaica shop which they never before had had, but now this!

"We expect more stock soon," Melech reassured, but the already upset Geshmak would not be placated, and he left the shop in a huff.

Meanwhile, during their several recent trips to Schmertzburg, Melech and Nasich had been invited to take tea and cake with Rebbe Dovid Plotzky, his wife and daughter, Dvorah. Nasich and Dvorah struck up a friendship, and in time, with the assistance of the Schmertzburg shadchan, a shidduch was arranged. The joy involved in the betrothal of the two young people on the part of the Liebeherz family, overcame any temporary annoyance or resentment expressed by Geshmak Feinkochen regarding the temporary paucity of inventory. Eventually, new stock arrived in both stores, and once again, all was well in the little shtetl of Patchentuch.

Naphtali Dreams

Gimpel Kvetchernick the shoemaker dreamed of shoes. Others may have dreamed of sugar plum fairies and such, but Gimpel dreamed only of shoes. Before he had married Bluma he dreamed of her as he flew in his dreams over ramshackle houses and fields and did somersaults in the air. So it was with his son Naphtali. Other Patchentuch sons may have dreamed of baked goods and barrels, but Naphtali's dreams like those of his father, were only of the shoes he would create. When *he* did loops de loops in his own dreams it was exclusively about the shoes he would design, and when he awoke he recorded these dreams on paper. His father had created the "sneakers, the loafers and the patent leathers," and so what was left for Naphtali to design on his own? After considerable thought concerning the matter he came to the realization that perhaps if he could not invent a new type of shoe he might be able to improve upon one of his father's creations.

Throughout all of his young life Naphtali had been surrounded by shoes, and at an early age had helped his father in the shoe shop. There were many sons of Patchentuch who were reluctant to follow in the footsteps of their fathers; these were the ones who struck out on their own to do something entirely different. For Naphtali, however, the aroma of shoe polish was an elixir. He enjoyed working along side his father whom he lionized, and who patiently taught him the trade. Of all the shoes Gimpel had designed, Naphtali's favorite was the "sneaker," which his father had created out of a canvas like material. Naphtali, an innovator himself, had been working on creating a slightly different fabric, similar to the "sneaker" fabric, but much lighter. It was the same material that cousin Lob Straub had so much admired on his visit to Patchentuch, and that his grandmother Rose

Kvetchernick used for the bags she made and still sold in the market, but considerably lighter in weight.

With pride Gimpel observed and encouraged his industrious son as Naphtali continued his experimentation with the strong but lighter fabric, and it reminded him of his own youthful excitement. Prototypes were made for the new "sneaker," and the results were encouraging. The fabric that Naphtali used to produce these particular "sneakers" was very light so that if one wished to run it would be much easier if one were wearing such shoes.

Naphtali called his innovative shoes "Naphtali's Running Shoes." When the time was right and the shoes were perfected, father and son sent off a sample to Harry, Barry and Larry (the former Hennoch, Benzion and Lochshen Cohen) in America. The Cohen brothers sought a market for such shoes, and they found a small company in America that bought them. Eventually, years later, when a larger company bought out this company, and another even larger company purchased that company, "Naphtali's Running Shoes" became "Nike," for short, and that is the long and the short of it.

Geshmak Trips

The Patchentuch law firm of Blum, Kapoyer and Rozencrantz had no business and never had. Whoever in this poor town could afford to pay them, anyway, even if they had a legitimate course of action? Moreover, since Chaim Kapoyer, one of the partners, was now the Mayor, he was occupied with town affairs that left him little time for lawyering. What extra time he had he spent making certain things were running smoothly in the family knife sharpening shop, now managed by his wife, Tovah.

As a result his law partners, Yitzhak Rozencrantz and Leybush Blum, both undertakers, felt abandoned. Until recently they had had frequent meetings with Chaim to discuss the law, but now that Chaim was Mayor there was little time for such things.

When one day Geshmak Feinkochen tripped and fell into a hole in the market square, he decided to sue the Town of Patchentuch for negligence, and he immediately attempted to retain the services of Blum, Kapoyer and Rozencrantz. It was the sacred responsibility of town government to tend to matters of street repair, and Geshmak claimed they had failed miserably. He brought the matter to the Mayor's attention while hobbling on a walking stick, and he informed Chaim of his intention to sue the town.

"This," he told the Mayor, "is not just a simple matter of stealing a knish, but of a far more serious nature. Because I have been injured, due to town negligence, I plan to bring legal action, and I wish to engage the services of your law firm in the matter of restitution for my injuries." Oy, thought Chaim to himself. If Geshmak brought charges against the town, of which he, Chaim, was a citizen and a resident, and his law firm represented Geshmak in this law suit against the town, then Chaim would, in effect, be suing himself.

How could it be that I will sue myself, he wondered, and at the thought he became confused in the extreme. He would either have to recuse himself, or resign from the firm, neither of which he wished to do. Moreover, his law partners were also citizens of the town, and they would, in effect, also be suing themselves, and the more Chaim thought about it, the more confused he became. Meanwhile Geshmak continued to rant and rave about the ineffectiveness of The Town Council and the Mayor, while Chaim consulted Leybush and Yitzhak, his law partners, regarding the matter. Moreover, a question of money was involved because the town could not afford to pay damages, nor could Blum, Kapoyer or Rozencrantz.

In the meantime, Faigele Scheinkopf, the town's urgent care person, was consulted by Geshmak regarding his injuries, but she told him it was no more than a slightly sprained ankle, which would soon heal, and so in the end it turned out to be no more than a "tempest in a teapot." The law firm would not take the case, and so Geshmak had no recourse. It became clear that a person could not sue himself, after all, and so the suit was dropped. Nevertheless, he continued to fume and fulminate, his ankle healed, the pot hole was filled, and the issue was eventually forgotten, until Geshmak found a new reason to complain, which is what he did better than anyone else in the poor little shtetl town of Patchentuch.

Sadie Considers Divorce

After thinking about it for many months and worrying what people would think, Sadie Schlepper decided that she no longer could stay married to her husband, Getzel. She, somewhat hesitantly, sought the help of the law firm of Blum, Kapoyer and Rozencrantz, who were reluctant to accept her case because it involved a possible conflict of interest, since Leybush Rozencrantz was related to Getzel Schlepper. Naturally, in the normal course of things the yentas learned of Sadie's plans to divorce Getzel, and when the community took sides in the affair it became manna for the gossip that spread rapidly through the Patchentuch community. It soon became a "cause celebre" prompting Sadie to consult Rebbe Benny, who had already heard of Sadie's decision. Rebbe Benny explained that divorce, and obtaining a "get" was no simple matter, and that it could be very time consuming and expensive. A law firm could not help her, nor could he. She would have to appeal to the Rabbinical Court in Warsaw to adjudicate and to resolve the situation.

How was Sadie to get to Warsaw, and where should she begin? She had no money for the trip, and so her idea of divorce began to appear less appealing and more complicated than she had imagined. She began to have thoughts regarding financial support and who would keep her warm on cold winter nights. Her grounds for divorce were that Getzel had complained about her cooking for so long that she had had enough. She would just have to find other ways to keep warm in bed on cold winter nights without him, and she would have to learn to fix broken things around the house. Her main grievance, however, was that Getzel could not stand her cooking, and that she had suffered enough of his complaints.

After her lengthy meeting with Rebbe Benny, however, Sadie

began to reconsider her options, which now appeared to be quite limited, and she came to the reluctant conclusion that divorce and procuring a "get" was too much bother, too expensive and far too complicated. After all, she was not young anymore, and perhaps the best solution would be to take cooking lessons from Fraidle Schmaltzberger, the best cook in Patchentuch, which is exactly what she did.

After awhile, Getzel no longer complained about Sadie's cooking, and perhaps, she thought, maybe she had been the problem all along. She would not get a get after all, which was probably not even necessary in the first place, had she paid any attention to her husband's complaints. One positive side benefit of the entire matter was that the law firm of Blum, Kapoyer and Rosencrantz could still claim that they had never lost a case.

Geshmak Pays A Visit

The success record of the Patchentuch law firm of Blum, Kapoyer and Rozencrantz was dismal, and the few inquiries that they had were of a frivolous nature. There had, for instance, been the issue when Geshmak Feinkochen had attended a Bar Mitzvah celebration in Schmertzburg, and the resident schnorrer of the town, Pinchas Dumkopf seized the last knish on a plate, just as Geshmak, who was an invited guest, was reaching for that very same knish. Geshmak was so insulted and distressed that he returned to Patchentuch ready to sue the town of Schmertzburg for negligent failure in controlling its schnorrer. The second case presented to the lawyers concerned the time when Geshmak had tripped and fallen in the market square and was prepared to sue the town of Patchentuch for its failure to maintain its streets in proper repair. As citizens of the town, the three lawyers were not prepared or willing to sue themselves, and so the case came to nothing. The third matter concerned the handling of Sadie Schlepper's proposed divorce proceedings. When it was learned that Leybish Rozencrantz was a cousin of Getzel Schlepper, Sadie's husband, the case was dismissed due to a conflict of interest.

Fate, it appeared, was denying opportunities for the success of the firm, causing the partners to become disheartened and discouraged, and so they began to entertain ideas of dissolving the partnership altogether.

When word reached Geshmak Feinkochen that Patchentuch might soon be losing its one and only law firm, the very firm that gave the town an advantage over Schmertzburg, he requested a meeting with the trio. It was a bright day with sunlight streaming through the windows, and all were present for the meeting, the subject of which was the prevention of a possible dissolution of the partnership. When all were assembled and ready for discussion of the issue, a large cloud floated across the sun causing the room to become suddenly dark. Leybish Rozencrantz thought he might be losing his eyesight, as did some of the others, but when the cloud passed and the room once again brightened, Geshmak saw this as a sign. He strongly urged against the dissolution of the firm, and that its members should hold fast, and he offered several reasons for this. Patchentuch would, sooner or later, need a lawyer, and their resilience and resolve would eventually be rewarded. Not that Geshmak was truly concerned about the welfare and success of the firm, nor the town. He only hoped that Patchentuch would not lose the edge it had always maintained over its neighbors in Schmertzburg, who had no law firm.

And so, the cloud passed, the sun came out, and because Geshmak was able to convince the group that it was a sign, the firm of Blum, Kapoyer and Rozencrantz remained in tact awaiting its first real case. Until then, however, Geshmak engaged them to draw up a will for him as their first legal action.

The Council Votes

When Moishe Kapoyer retired as Mayor of Patchentuch for the fourth and final time, most of the members of his Council remained to provide their "help and guidance" to the new Mayor, Chaim Kapoyer, son of the former Mayor. They soon discovered, however, that Chaim neither thought about nor needed their thought or guidance. Instead, he sought younger people to fill Council seats, and he thanked the Council profusely for their many years of service; he even organized a party in celebration in honor of their long service. "Long" is the operative word as most of the Council members had served since Moishe became Mayor, and like Moishe, they had aged for over the many years of Moishe's tenure in office.

At the celebration, Schmendric Teitlebaum, the longest serving Council member, at the request of his colleagues made a speech.

"My friends, we seven old men have served you as members of the Patchentuch Town Council for so many years that none of us can remember how long ago that was. I recall only that when I first joined the Council my eldest son Avraham was just a baby. Now he is a grandfather himself. I am not sure of his age, but look at him sitting there with his family, and that should tell you how long my friends and I have served on the Council. That should also tell you," he continued, "that it has come time for us to yield our seats to younger men who are familiar with modern life and the needs of a growing and changing town. I can tell you," Schmendric continued, "that in the old days. . ." and he rambled on and on, until one brave soul, sensing that the speech might go on forever, and that he had to get up for work in the morning, stood and shouted,

"So let's have a shnappes and a toast to all our retiring members of the Town Council, and let us say, "Hip, hip, hooray," and everyone quickly stood and shouted, "Hip, hip, hooray," except for the other, now former Council members, who were enjoying Schmendric's speech.

When Mayor Chaim Kapoyer selected the six new members of his Council he did his best to balance the "left" (the progressives) with the "right" (the traditionalists,) and so he chose three on each side. Two of the new Council members, Pinchas Plotz and Gimmel Lochinkopf, who seldom thought the same way, ran the Patchentuch Book Store together, and as a result they spent a good deal more time in each others company than did other Council members. In the store Pinchas and Gimmel shared many hours discussing local issues, and because each had a different opinion from the other, they enjoyed many good natured debates, as well. Recently, while mulling over an issue that had arisen regarding the relocation of the post office, Gimmel convinced Pinchas that they should vote together on the issue, and that moving the location was the logical and sensible thing to do. In this instance Gimmel brought Pinchas around to his way of thinking, but then the philosophical balance that the Mayor had sought in his Council, would shift. The Mayor would then not be required to cast the deciding vote which was the case with the usual and predictable tie.

This was certain to upset Mayor Chaim Kapoyer, because most votes usually ended in a tie, allowing him to cast the deciding vote, which was frequently on the side of caution, rather than progress. Thus, the progressives did not usually get their way because Chaim, by virtue of his tie breaking vote, assured that tradition would rule in Patchentuch. Most people were comfortable with things as they were, however, and the idea of change was daunting. Like his father before him, Chaim was a traditionalist to whom the idea of significant change was anathema. The Jews of Patchentuch were essentially a traditional people who comfortably clung to their time honored customs and beliefs. Any innovation that involved forward thinking ideas or any form of change made them uneasy, and so when a shift in location of the post office was brought to the floor of the Council Chamber, Chaim was concerned.

For years the post office had been housed in Maisy and Getzel

Prochnik's Dry Goods Store, but in a growing town, the store was frequently too crowded. Thus, a new and larger location for the location for the post office was found, but the thought of such a change upset some residents. They liked the post office where it had always been, crowded or not. On this particular issue Pinchas and Gimmel were now of like mind. A larger location was indeed necessary, and if these two Council members voted the same way, a tie breaking vote would not be required by the Mayor, and he would not have the final say, as he always had. If in the future, other Council coalitions were formed, Chaim's vote could remain unnecessary and his control of the Council would be lost.

The Mayor tossed and turned in his bed at night worrying about such matters. Why would a Mayor be needed if a Council could decide everything, and how might that affect life in the town. It would be a drastic change, for sure, and people would complain to him as they inevitably did. In the meantime, discussions in the Council continued involving all the pros and cons of moving the post office. Chaim, himself, was not in favor of a change, but now, he might be denied the deciding vote that he wanted, and all because of the recent news that Gimmel Lochinkopf had persuaded Pinchas Plotz to vote his way. Because the dynamic had changed, Mayor Chaim Kapoyer continued to toss and turn in his bed at night and could not sleep.

After too much discussion regarding the change of venue of the Patchentuch Post Office, the day of the final vote arrived. The sleep-deprived Mayor was relieved that it was time for the issue to be resolved one way or the other, and not surprisingly, his tie breaking vote was not required, a vote which would have ordinarily annoyed half of his Council anyway, as it most often did. As it turned out, in a vote of four to two, the Council voted in favor of a post office relocation, and even the Mayor was relieved. Perhaps, after all, it would not really be such a bad thing, and everyone would, sooner or later, become accustomed to the newer and better location, and after that Mayor Chaim Kapoyer slept like a baby, at least for the time being.

A Match Made In Heaven

The two members of Patchentuch's Chevra Kaddisha, The Burial Society, were bachelors. Apparently, young women were reluctant to marry undertakers, and so Yitzhak Rozencrantz and Leybush Blum had been unable to find wives. Even the village shadchan had found it too great a challenge, and so the two men remained unmarried, and without wives and children to provide distraction from their sad, but noble work. To the disappointment of their mothers, the men still lived at home. Friends and relatives had tried to arrange a shidduch for them but nothing had ever worked out. Studying and discussing the law had provided somewhat of a distraction, but their law firm, Blum, Kapoyer and Rozencrantz had few clients, with the recent exception of Geshmak Feinkochen for whom they had drawn up a will.

* * * * *

Some time ago a visitor to the town had rented a room in Hester Britchky's Shtetl Betl. He said he had traveled from Lublin to visit a relative. During his brief stay he was befriended by the Britchkys, and they were sorry to see him go when he finally left for home. His name was Shmul Leibele, and when he recently reappeared in town to attend to some business, he once again stayed with the Britchkys. During his previous visit he had learned that a law firm existed in the town, a firm whose services he now wished to engage to draw up a will. Having no immediate family of his own, (contrary to what he had told the Britchys on his last visit) he intended to leave all he possessed to his two nieces, Fruma and Fraida Plotzky.

When Shmul Leibele visited the law office of Blum, Kapoyer and Rozencrantz, Leybush and Yitzhak were there, and it is with them that he discussed the terms of the bequests. Having recently created a will for Geshmak Feinkochen, the men were now familiar with the process. Accordingly, they drafted the document that Shmul Leibele required, naming Fruma and Fraida as his only beneficiaries, and stipulating that the two ladies pay a visit to their office to sign appropriate documents. They set a date and time for the signing, following which the firm's second official client left for home.

Some time later, the nieces, Fruma and Fraida Plotzky visited the law office of Blum, Kapoyer and Rozencrantz to sign the required papers. When they originally received the notice of their inheritance, they were perplexed. Neither one had any idea that they had a relative named Shmul Leibele, and so they were understandably confused. When they journeyed to Patchentuch for the meeting, they met with Leybush and Yitzhak, who explained it all to them. Both signed the appropriate papers confirming that they would receive the bequest of this unknown relative who had been so generous. A second, (and perfectly unnecessary) meeting was arranged by the lawyers, who had taken a fancy to the young ladies, and because fate worked in strange ways, not very long afterward, after several more unnecessary meetings, a double engagement was announced in Patchentuch.

In due course Leybush married Fruma, and Yitzhak married Fraida, and all the while the identity of the unknown benefactor remained a mystery. It was many years ago, when Shmul Leibele had first visited Patchentuch, claiming to be a cousin to a person who was, in fact, no relation at all, that curiosity regarding the mysterious visitor was aroused. When Tevya Minevitz, the shadchan, and erstwhile mystic, heard the stories of how the visit of the stranger had resulted in a beneficial reversal of fortunes for the Britchkys, and now, the betrothal of the long time bachelor undertakers, he intuitively suspected that Shmul Leibele might be an angel of God. That is why in the Hebrew scriptures according to Leviticus, (and to Tevya,) it is written that it is incumbent upon us all to welcome the stranger in our midst, because one never knows if or when an angel of the Lord would come to visit.

In the end, Yitzhak and Leybush married their bashert, moved out of their parents' homes, had families of their own, and were happy just continuing to serve the good people of the little shtetl of Patchentuch.

Fruma and Fraida Arrive

Upon the marriages of the two undertaker/lawyers, Leybush Rozencrantz and Yitzhak Blum, there was much excitement in Patchentuch. Curiosity regarding the new brides, the former Fruma and Fraida Plotzky, was rife, especially among the yentas, and the community was prepared to welcome them into their midst. Moreover, there was much speculation regarding who Yitzhak and Leybush had chosen to marry. According to rumor the men had made the acquaintance of the women through their client at Blum, Kapoyer and Rozencrantz. The mysterious Shmul Leibel, a purported uncle, had visited the office for the purpose of drawing up a will designating the two young women as beneficiaries.

* * * * *

After the wedding celebration, the couples settled into their new homes, and the town's residents were introduced to the young women, now the wives of their undertaker/lawyers. It was eventually discovered that Fruma and Fraida had a business of their own, The Plotzky Puppets of Patchentuch, similar to the business of the Pulkes Puppets, managed by Chatchkel Pulkes. Apparently, and to everyone's surprise, Patchentuch would now claim the distinction of having two puppet theaters compared to the neighboring town of Schmertzburg which had none. (Naturally, when Geshmak Feinkochen learned about this, he was delighted, because it was he who was obsessed with such things.) In addition, and according to the yentas, the exclusivity that Chatchkel had always enjoyed as the town's only puppeteer might now be in jeopardy. Because of his unique puppet shows, a kind of celebrity in the town was accorded him, and now there might be competition.

"So what will happen?" asked Ida Finklestein.

"What do you mean what will happen?" responded Essa Bissel.

"Now that we have competing puppeteers in the town, will they speak?"

"Of course they'll speak," Faigele Scheinkopf assured the yentas. "They may even like one another and become friends," and eventually, to the disappointment of the most fervent yentas, that is what happened. There was never a competition at all, and, in fact, and over time, a strong and lasting friendship developed.

* * * * *

No one had really known much about Fruma and Fraida, but what the yentas and others learned, was that back in Lublin, where the women had lived, their mother died at a relatively young age. As a result, the daughters were raised by their father, a professional puppeteer. Accordingly, he had taught the girls the art of puppetry, and from a young age they learned how to build marionettes, to dress them, and how to work them. As they grew, Fruma and Fraida became expert in the art, and as the fame and reputation of The Plotzky Puppets grew, so did the joy and pleasure, especially on the part of the children of Lublin, spread.

When their father died, and the girls, now young women, were left alone, they supported themselves through their art, and they continued to be loved by the children of their town. Now, years later, when they were living in Patchentuch, and happily married to their undertaker/lawyer husbands, they brought that same joy into their own homes, where they lightened the heavy burdens of their husbands.

Before they met Chatchel Pulkes, issues of a competition had been raised, but because they all had so much in common they eventually combined their talents and abilities to become The Pulkes and Plotzsky Puppets. They shared stories, techniques and all of the many skills they had respectively honed over the years, and together they designed new sets and scenery for their shows whose reputation spread far and wide.

* * * * *

When years later Fruma and her sister Fraida received a monetary bequest from their anonymous benefactor, they invested some of the money toward improvements in their joint puppet theater. Their reputation grew, and their performances continued to spread joy and laughter throughout the region, a fact which caused Shmul Leibel, wherever and whoever he was, to smile.

Chaim's Legacy

As the new Mayor of Patchentuch, Chaim Kapoyer was determined to leave a legacy and to make his mark. He hoped that he might be remembered with the same admiration and respect accorded his now retired father, the previous Mayor. Notwithstanding that his father, Moishe Kapoyer, had once constructed an upside down house because he had read the plans and instructions upside down, he was, and had always been regarded with love and reverence. Chaim simply wanted to achieve the same exalted status as his father, and he hoped to be remembered for being more than just a Mayor who saw to it that potholes were filled and mud was removed from streets and lanes. He dreamed about achieving a worthy accomplishment, something that would remain as the hallmark of his tenure as Mayor of Patchentuch. Thus far into his term he had dealt only with potholes and mud, trifling squabbles between neighbors, and other matters of a trivial nature. A library had been established in Patchentuch, as well as a bank and a law firm, not to mention that an additional well had been dug, but this had all occurred under his father's watch. What would be left for him, Chaim Kapoyer, to achieve that would be remembered as a significant accomplishment of his administration?

When not otherwise occupied Chaim spent hours pondering ways for him to leave his mark, but without success, until one day it occurred to him that the town of Patchentuch did not have, nor had ever had a Municipal Government Center. Over the years the Mayor and his Council had always met in a vacant house off the Market Square, a somewhat dilapidated building that sadly needed more than just a coat of paint. They met in a cramped meeting room in a building clearly not worthy of housing the office of a Mayor. Even Schmertzburg had a more formidable Municipal Government

Center, (a fact, by the way, not overlooked by Geshmak Feinkochen.) How such an embarrassing oversight had been allowed to exist for so long confounded Chaim. It was a shanda and an insult to the respectability of the Town of Patchentuch and its citizens, and he would undertake to do something about it.

At the next Council meeting Chaim raised the subject of establishing a Patchentuch Municipal Government Center, a new building that would define their town as a place of importance and significance. With such a building Patchentuch would not be just any old shtetl town among many, but a place of importance, known for a Municipal Government Center of grandeur, a place to which people would be drawn in connection with important matters of town governance. For too long a ramshackle building had been the face of town government, and if it was up to Chaim Kapoyer that would soon change. Such a new building would put Patchentuch on the map, and to this end Mayor Chaim Kapoyer presented his case to the Council.

"So why do we need such a center?" asked Beymish Schmootz.

"Yes, why?" echoed Yossel Fartumelt, followed by Pinchas Plotz who was concerned about financing such an ambitious venture. Much questioning, some of it very loud, followed before Chaim had an opportunity to respond.

"Perhaps it is something we should consider," interrupted Gimmel Lochinkopf.

"It is an interesting thought," Gideon Koach added, and Tevya Helfen agreed with Gimmel and Gideon that the idea had merit. As usual the Council was split down the middle, and more vociferous debate ensued. Those who were against the idea shouted down those who were in favor of considering a new and better Municipal Government Center, (perhaps because it was a "new" idea.) At the risk of appearing self serving Chaim was reluctant to interfere in the heated debate. (He had apparently forgotten the lessons he had learned, and the instruction regarding assertiveness he had received from his wife, mother- in- law and daughter,) and so the final conclusion appeared to admit that the poor shtetl town of

Patchentuch could not afford the expenditure for such a building. The most they could all agree to was a fresh coat of paint for the building, and Chaim would be obliged to abide by the Council's decision. That, however, would not stop him from dreaming about a future when he might accomplish something grand, something to provide the town with a noble and lasting legacy. Everyone needed a dream, something toward which to aspire, and Mayor Chaim Kapoyer would hold fast to his own special dream, which one day might very well become a reality... but only time would tell.

The Mayor Persists

Mayor Chaim Kapoyer was disappointed that his hopes for creating a new municipal building for the town of Patchentuch had met with disapproval. No one on the Town Council agreed with his proposal for a new and improved Municipal Government Center, and after much heated discussion the idea was tabled. The only concession that Chaim succeeded in obtaining was agreement to paint the ramshackle building that presently housed the Council Meeting Room as well as the Mayor's office.

For days Chaim "licked his wounds," and quietly suffered the criticism of his family regarding the fact that he had not been more assertive. His wife, Fruma, was especially harsh in her judgement in view of the assertiveness training she, her mother and daughter had given Chaim. Be that as it may, if the only concession that had been granted was to paint the existing building, then so be it. Chaim would engage the services of a group of Polish laborers who were repairing potholes in the Market Square, while he himself would select the paint. Leaving that decision to his Council would only result in lengthy and fruitless discussion and argument, of which Chaim had had his fill for the time being. The members had agreed to painting the building, which was affordable and long past due, and so Chaim went to work before they changed their minds.

To this end he went to select the paint, and after being shown several colors Chaim made his choice. The color of the existing building had always been brown, but according to Chaim's way of thinking, the color did not make much of a statement. It was dull and drab and without character, and it needed and deserved a fresh coat of paint at last. After examining several samples of paint he settled on a bright shade of yellow, a strong color of character that made a statement. People looking for The Patchentuch Town Hall would now surely be able to locate it. The color would be unique and would command attention, no longer becoming lost in a sea of ubiquitous brown. Accordingly, Chaim thought, by selecting such a strong color of character, people would sit up and take notice of the Town Hall. It would no longer be just another drab brown building lost in a drab landscape. Because of the bright new color it might even become something of a monument, set apart from the rest of the town, and so Chaim ordered the paint.

When the paint was mixed and ready, and the laborers had completed their work with the potholes, they began painting the Town Hall. Unfortunately, the disappointing result was that when the work was done, people said that it looked like a giant jar of mustard resting by the Market Square. It was ugly and unsightly they said, and regarding the newly painted structure a collective "oy" was heard throughout the town of Patchentuch. It was such an eyesore that Tovah, Chaim's wife, also agreed that it was a most unfortunate choice of color, and she convinced her husband to meet with his Council members, who were also complaining.

"How about red?" suggested a clueless Yossel Fartumel, and so they repainted the building red. The problem was that when the red paint mixed with the yellow color, which had not yet set, it turned to orange.

"How about blue?" suggested Pinchas Plotz, and so they repainted the building blue. The problem was that when the blue mixed with the still wet orange it turned to bright green.

"How about using up the extra red paint that is left and repainting it red and see what happens this time," suggested Beymish Schmootz, and so they used up all the red paint that remained. The problem was that when the red mixed with the still damp green it all turned to brown once again.

"How about we paint it black," Gideon suggested, in frustration.

"Black? Are you crazy?" they all exclaimed, and so because no one could agree on a color, the Polish workers quit and left, and in the end the building remained brown as it had always been.

The Mayor's Decision

Chaim Kapoyer took his role as Mayor very seriously. His wife, Tovah, was aware of this, and because she wanted him to succeed, she and her mother Shayna, Chaim's mother- in- law, decided to give Chaim additional lessons in assertiveness. To this end they arranged more training sessions so that when at Council meetings Chaim would be better prepared to assert himself, if need be. Of course, it never occurred to Chaim that the Council was only there for the benefit of their thinking and advice, and he, the Mayor did not really need their vote at all.

After the most recent training sessions Chaim, in appreciation for their efforts on his behalf, volunteered to pick up groceries at the market for his wife and mother- in- law. Having never ever spent much time in the market place, he was struck by the sight of so many old women struggling with heavy baskets on their arms. It was clearly difficult for them at their age, and it gave Chaim an idea. He knew that Leibish Liebowitz, the now retired milkman, owned a cart and a donkey, and so later that week he paid the old man a visit. After greeting Leibish and asking after him and his wife Mathilda, and their general well being, he told him of an idea that had come to him in the market place.

"Do you still own your milk cart and donkey, Leibish?" Chaim asked.

"Yes, I still have my cart and my Bathsheba," he told the Mayor.

"And what do you to keep active during your retirement?" he asked Leibish.

"A little of this and a little of that," Leibish said.

"So here is an idea I would like to share with you.

"You have an idea?"

"Yes, I have an idea, and this is what it is. How would you like to offer your services every Monday and Thursday on market days each week?"

"Doing what?" Leibish asked.

"Driving home the old women with their groceries in your wagon. It would be a mitzvah, Leibish, and if you agree you will be paid a small amount to provide this service for the old mothers and grandmothers of our town." Leibish listened to the Mayor's proposal, and after consulting Mathilda, he realized it was a good idea, for himself as well as for the old women of the town, and he agreed to perform such a service.

After his meeting with Leibish, and at the very next Council meeting Chaim presented his idea, requesting a small fund to support this service which would be a mitzvah for the town, and especially for the old women of Patchentuch, the mothers and the grandmothers.

"Oy," remarked Beymish Schmootz upon hearing the Mayor's proposal. "More money we should spend, money that we do not have to spare?"

"Yes, our funds are dangerously low," agreed Yossel Fartumelt.

"Our funds may be low," echoed Gimmel Lochinkopf, "but there are priorities."

"Never mind priorities," blurted out Pinchas Plotz, "there are also limits."

"So all of a sudden you don't care about old ladies?" countered Gideon Koach.

"Of course I care about old ladies. Everybody cares about old ladies," responded Pinchas.

"But you don't care enough," shouted Tevya Helfen.

"We care about a lot of things but we cannot afford to pay for all of these things that we care about," Pinchas told the group, and the arguments in favor of old ladies, and against incurring new expenditures continued, until finally Chaim interrupted.

"Enough already," he shouted. "I have heard enough. I value and respect your thoughts, opinions and input, which always influence the decisions that I make. In this particular case, however, I have heard your voices and listened to your arguments, and I have made the decision to fund this project. Minimal funds will be allotted, but in the name of kindness, humanity and consideration for our oldest citizens, our mothers and grandmothers, it is incumbent upon us to support the project.

Because of the Mayor's assertive insistence, funds were made available to pay Leibish for carting home the old women of Patchentuch every Monday and Thursday. The children of the town patted Bathsheba as she drew the old ladies home with their groceries in the wagon that Leibish drove. As a sign of appreciation and recognition for what their Mayor had done for the old people of the town, Chatchkel Pulkes, the woodcarver and puppeteer, carved a special wooden sign which was affixed to the front of the newly painted Town Hall, and it read "Patchentuch Municipal Building, Chaim Kapoyer, Mayor," and so Chaim's legacy had begun, along with a new respect by the Council for the wisdom of their Mayor.

By the way, in the end, and in the spirit of good will, Leibish declined to accept any money for his services, and all was well in the little town of Patchentuch.

Mathilda Is Worried

Ever since Leibish Liebowitz had begun to provide transportation for Patchentuch's old ladies from the market to their homes, a great burden had been lifted from many aching shoulders. As the old women sat together in Leibish's wagon, and Bathsheba pulled them toward their homes, they happily kibbitzed. No longer were they required to carry heavy baskets to their homes from the market, nor to slog through mud and snow, but instead they were able to comfortably sit in the wagon and chat.

At his own insistence Leibish was not paid for his services, but he performed them as a mitzvah for the older residents of the town, something he was proud to do. Occasionally the old women would bring him cakes that they had baked, or they would slip him a zloty or two. The cakes he and Mathilda enjoyed, but the zlotys Leibish kept in a special glass jar. It gave Mayor Chaim Kapoyer much pleasure and satisfaction to have been responsible for having made such a service possible for the town's elderly citizens, and even the Mayor's Council enjoyed the reflected glory.

Over time, the number of zlotys in Leibish's glass jar had grown, but he did not touch them. He just enjoyed looking at them and watching them grow in number. One day, when Mathilda was doing her dusting, she noticed that the level of coins in the jar was considerably lower than it had been. It was obvious that the jar was now less than one quarter full, whereas the last time she looked it had been nearly full. Memories of Leibish's past gambling habits crept into the corners of her mind, and she remembered when Shleppy Teitlebaum from the bank had loaned Leibish the money to pay off a gambling debt. In exchange for the loan, the bank took ownership of Bathsheba, and not until the loan was repaid, which it was, would ownership of their beloved donkey be returned. Mathilda shuddered at the thought that Leibish, after all these years, had slipped back into his old ways, God forbid.

Fortunately, and not long after, and before any damage was done, Leibish surprised his wife with a shiny new cooking utensil, a large pot with a cover that he bought for her as a present from his zloty collection. Upon receipt of the shiny new pot, Mathilda immediately burst into tears, hugged her husband and thanked him for his generosity and thoughtfulness. Of course, unknown to Leibish, her tears were mostly due to profound relief, and that very night she cooked her husband a special dish in her shiny new pot. Bathsheba was never in any danger of repossession by the bank because Liebish was truly reformed, and Mathilda knew it.

Shlomo Lochinkopf's Sons

Shlomo and Raizel Lochinkopf were the parents of six sons, and because Shlomo had always been severely memory challenged, he feared that one day he might even forget the names of his own children. In that regard, and years ago, he began by naming his first child, a son, Aleph. When his second son was born Shlomo named him Bet, and ultimately his six sons bore the names of the first six letters of the Hebrew alphabet. His third son, Gimmel, now ran a bookstore in Patchentuch with Pinchas Plotz, and his sixth, and youngest son, Vov, had emigrated to Palestine to join his own son, Zion.

Aleph, the oldest, was an idealist who wished only to better society and mankind, and when he once attended a meeting promoting rights and privileges for all citizens of the country, he got himself into some trouble. Subsequently, he left for Palestine, where he joined his brother Vov and his nephew, Zion. Now two of Shlomo's sons resided in the "Land of Their Fathers," leaving behind their old parents and their brothers Bet, Gimmel, Dalet and Hey.

Vov and Aleph sent letters back home to the family wherein they expressed their sense of fulfillment in working to rebuild the land of the Jewish people. The letters reassured the family that they were well, happy and fulfilled, but these letters planted a seed in the minds of the brothers who remained in Patchentuch. The letters spoke of the warmth and the sunshine, while the brothers at home continued to endure long, cold winters and the hardships of Patchentuch lives.

Gimmel Lochinkopf, who served on the Mayor's Council and ran a bookstore in Patchentuch with Pinchas Plotz, a fellow Council member, was envious of his two intrepid chalutz (pioneer) brothers who worked the land in the sunshine and warmth of Palestine, and he shared these feelings with his brothers Bet, Dalet and Hey. From the letters they all sensed that their "Sabra" brothers were living meaningful lives in the rebuilding of a land and establishing a home for the scattered Jews of the world who never had a secure place to really call their home. When the brothers shared their thoughts with their now old father, Shlomo worried. Raizel, however, understood that there was no future security in a Patchentuch life, and she reassured her husband.

"What will be will be," she told him. "Do not worry," and so Shlomo forgot to worry as he forgot most everything else. Eventually, Aleph, Bet, Gimmel, Dalet, Hey and Vov all ended up in the "Land of Their Fathers," helping to rebuild the country of the Jewish people.

* * * * *

With the unexpected departure of Gimmel Lochinkopf, however, Mayor Chaim Kapoyer now found himself short one member of his Council, which was just another added headache with which to deal.

Chaim's Predicament

Mayor Chaim Kapoyer was in the process of finding a Council member to replace Gimmel Lochinkopf who had left for Palestine. A farewell party was thrown for Gimmel and his brothers, who also emigrated, and off they all went. In an attempt to maintain philosophical balance on the board, Chaim was left with the task of finding a new and qualified member to join his Council, someone with a similar philosophical bent to that of Gimmel, a person with somewhat of a progressive leaning.

To this end he considered several potential candidates for the position, such as Perchik Schmaltzberger, grandson of Zelig, who had previously expressed some interest. Unfortunately, Perchik had often demonstrated some of the absent mindedness and ineptitude of his grandfather, and so Chaim discounted his potential candidacy. Yossel Plotz, a drayman and younger brother of Pinchas, had been another possibility, but he had never really expressed much interest in the position. Binyamin Walensky had seemed like another possibility, but he was so lost in his spiritual and scholarly studies that he would surely be incapable of dealing with mundane matters of mud and potholes. The same was true of Bezalel Guta, the tallis maker and son of Nisht Guta, and so, in frustration, Chaim abandoned his search which had proven to be futile and frustrating. Eventually he began to think that perhaps in this particular situation less might be more, and to this end he decided to settle for what he had. When Pinchas Plotz, however, suddenly made the decision to leave the Council because of added responsibilities in the bookstore because of Gimmel's emigration to Palestine, Chaim made a final decision. If there were fewer members on the board, there would be fewer people to engage in controversy and dispute, which might be a good thing.

There would still be balance in thought, and, of course, Chaim, in this case, would always have the deciding vote. Perhaps that is how it should have been in the first place. Knowing Patchentuch's people as he did, he understood that they would always hold strong opinions that they were not reluctant to share, and so perhaps this new dynamic would be a godsend. Chaim could only hope.

The Question Of the Tallis

When the old tallis maker of Patchentuch, Lochshen Kugel, retired, his apprentice, Nisht Guta, replaced him. Having trained and worked with Lochshen for many years, Nisht, himself, was now an expert. Years later, Nisht's two now grown sons followed in their father's footsteps becoming tallis makers themselves. According to orthodox Jewish tradition the tallis, or prayer shawl, was to be only worn by men, and when Betzalel, one of Nisht's sons was asked by his wife, Sima, to make her a tallis, Betzalel refused. Traditionally, women were not permitted to wear a tallis, and when Netta, wife of Naphtali, Betzalel's brother, also expressed a desire to wear a tallis at prayers, both Guta brothers were upset.

Somehow word spread regarding the desire of the two Guta wives to wear a tallis at prayers, and suddenly requests, and even orders from other women began to trickle in. That is when the controversy became a "cause celebre" in the town, and because the issue concerned civil rights in a way, Mayor Chaim Kapoyer and his Council found themselves involved. Rebbe Benny Rachmanes also joined the conversation, but his take on the controversy was strictly traditional, as one would expect. Women simply did not wear a tallis. Nevertheless, the women of the town continued to raise a hue and cry. They argued that it was time for a change, and why would it be such a terrible thing if women were permitted to wear a prayer shawl at prayers? Would it really be so awful? Why just the men?

"You want to wear a shawl?" the men asked. "Fine," they agreed, "wear a shawl, but not a tallis. The knots, patterns and fringes of a tallis have religious significance, but importantly there is the issue of tradition and law."

"We are just as Jewish as you are," the women responded, "and this is blatant discrimination, and just plain unfair. Our Judaism means as much to us as it does to you," they continued to argue, "and there is no good reason at all for exclusion in this regard."

A kind of war of the sexes ultimately broke out in the town, and people took sides in the heated debate. Rebbe Benny was under siege from the resentful women, moreover, husbands and wives were not speaking. The women were adamant, as were the men, until at last, before domestic turmoil became worse, and the situation deteriorated any further, a decision was reached by the Mayor. The services of the law firm of Blum, Kapoyer and Rozencrantz was engaged, and a trial would be held. Twelve jurors were selected, and the case involving a woman's right to wear a tallis was subsequently argued before the jury.

* * * * *

In the end the traditionalists won (after all, this was still Patchentuch). Thus, Netta and Sima were not allowed to wear a tallis in shul, and domestic tranquility was restored, (or almost restored,) in the little town of Patchentuch. The women might have been comforted had they known that one day in the not too distant future, their great granddaughters would be able to freely worship in shul with a tallis draped around their shoulders, if they so wished. For now, however, they would behave, and they would abide by the rules. The jury's decision contained no mandates, however, that women had to be happy about it.

The Yentatas

Albeit reluctantly, Sima and Netta Guta accepted the court's ruling that, according to tradition, only men were allowed to wear a tallis (tzizit, or fringes.) There were many other young women in the town of Patchentuch, however, who, unlike Sima and Netta, the two wives of the tallis makers, were unwilling to accept the court's decision with good grace. Times had begun to change, and they were upset and resentful that women had been treated so badly by the judgement in the matter of wearing the tallis.

These daughters of the "yentas," were known as "yentatas," yentas in training, who were, for the most part, somewhat more forward thinking than their mothers, and they bitterly resented the restrictions and limitations placed upon them just because they were women. The most vocal women in the group were Hannah Plotz, wife of Pinchas, Bayla Fartumelt, wife of Yossel and Faigel Schmaltzberger, wife of Perchik. These young women continually chafed and strained against the restrictions placed upon them, prohibitions which to them appeared archaic, as well as discriminatory, and they decided to do something about it. One day they might have daughters of their own who would expect more for women. They spoke of similar things as did their mothers, but recently they expanded their repertoire of topics beyond the sharing of recipes. When they met together they usually brought knitting with them, and as they chatted and knit, a wicked thought occurred to Hannah Plotz which she shared with the others.

"The men have informed us that we are "permitted" to wear shawls," she said to her friends.

"Yes, so what about it?" asked Bayla. "We have always worn

shawls, and for that we have never needed anyone's permission," and they all laughed.

"Thank God," they uttered in unison.

"Yes, thank God for small blessings," they agreed.

"We love our men, but, oy," Hannah Plotz remarked before sharing her idea. "Why don't we knit ourselves the shawls that we are "permitted" to wear, but without fringes, of course. We can knit our shawls with white wool, adding stripes of blue, just like the tallis, but without the required knotted fringes."

"And what will we do with these white shawls with blue stripes that we each will knit?" asked Bayla Fartumelt.

"We will wear them to shul every Shabbos, and we will be doing exactly what the men have given us "permission" to do. We will follow and scrupulously obey the rules that they have laid down for us. We will be wearing a tallis, that will not really be a tallis because it will be knitted, and it will have no fringes, and there is not a thing they can do about it…. and that is exactly what they did.

* * * * *

When the white wool shawls with the blue stripes were knit and had no fringes, the women proudly draped them over their shoulders at prayers in shul on Shabbos, and they felt vindicated, and there was nothing anyone could do about it, and that was the end of that… period. Of course, the men grumbled, but that was music to the ears of the Yentatas.

Melech And Darwin

Not only were the "Yentatas" a continuing irritant to the many traditionalists of Patchentuch, but, at times, also was Melech Liebeherz. After all, Melech was highly self educated, who was known as a well read and informed scholar. He was familiar with both the religious texts, and well as the secular texts, including the writings of Franz Kafka and Charles Darwin. For this very reason Melech was sometimes considered a threat to the extremely religious of the town. It was feared that he might influence and corrupt the young people, as well as create doubters of the old, especially when it came to a subject like evolution, which was never discussed. Few, if any in Patchentuch, had ever heard of evolution, and if they had heard, the information was discounted as fiction at best, or at worse, heresy. According to Charles Darwin, over millions of years man had evolved from monkeys, and such an idea was anathema to the Orthodox Jews of Patchentuch. The mindset of the people in Patchentuch was rooted in the belief that God had created the world in six days, leaving the creation of Man for his crowning achievement. The idea that it could all be metaphor did not factor into their thinking, except, that is, for the thinking of Melech Liebeherz.

"Can it really be true that we were once monkeys?" inquired those who had heard it from Melech, and when others learned that they were the descendants of monkeys, a hue and cry was raised in the town. At one time Melech had explained to some residents about gravity, but *this* was beyond the pale. Mothers began to worry that if their young children were to hear such nonsense they would become frightened. God created Man, and that was that. God did not create Man as a monkey who swung from trees and made terrible screeching noises. Children could be traumatized by such fables, and so the parents of young children paid a hurried visit to Rebbe Benny, where they shared their concerns.

"Oy, Rebbe," they complained, "Melech is telling our children that they were once monkeys, and the children are coming home crying, insisting that they are not monkeys."

"This cannot be happening," Rebbe Benny assured the anxious parents."

"Well it is," they told him. Granted, Melech was a teacher and an educator, but this new information was contrary to anything they had ever learned, and against what they had always believed in their hearts and souls. Regarding the Creation, all they knew was that the Lord had created the world in six days, and on that last day he created Man, who was definitely not a monkey.

When word spread further throughout the shtetl that Melech was teaching about "natural selection," all hell broke loose, so to speak. Melech was severely reprimanded, especially by the parents of young and impressionable children, and from that time on, he tried to keep his thoughts and views to himself. If someone came to him seeking answers to difficult questions regarding such subjects as gravity or monkeys, he would provide them with the answers they sought, but only if they promised not to tell. He had come to understand that the people of Patchentuch, whom he loved, and for whom he had great affection, the time was not yet right for the lessons he would like to impart. It would require future generations to accept such information, but for now, he was patient and hopeful.

Patchentuch Learns To Swim

Modern concepts and ideas excited Melech Liebeherz; they did not alarm him. Conversely, most Patchentuch residents were comfortable with the old ways, and they were fearful of change. It was only through his research and and studying that Melech had acquired his knowledge of the world, but because his community was essentially isolated from the modern world, most residents clung to the narrow religious traditions which they had known all of their lives. Notwithstanding that Melech had agreed to keep his counsel regarding the subject of evolution, which had caused near hysteria in the town, rumors spread that Melech had casually remarked that even before mankind evolved from monkeys, men were fish. Apparently, according to Melech, certain fish life from the ocean had once, millions of years ago, landed upon shore, where over time it developed a form of webbed feet, and the evolutionary process continued from there. Those who heard the stories naturally assumed that if men were fish before they were monkeys, these men must have an instinctive ability to swim without any special instruction whatsoever.

Because of this flawed reasoning, during the summer months some Patchentuch non-swimmers walked to the banks of the Tuches River and jumped in. Of course, the results were disastrous when many of these residents came perilously close to drowning. No one had thought to first consult Schlamazel Lifshutz, who could not swim, but was known to have once taken a bath in the river while also doing his laundry, and had tripped and was nearly swept away by the current. Where were those innate fish swimming skills he was supposed to have been born with? He might have warned others, had he been consulted, that he clearly had not inherited the purported swimming skills of their "fish" forebears. Fortunately, no one drowned in the river, but many were disappointed to discover that they had not been born with a natural ability to swim.

After several close calls, some Patchentuch residents finally decided to take swimming lessons. The task fell upon the beekeeper, Gershom Nussbaum, who had, himself, once nearly drowned when he jumped into the river in order to escape a swarm of angry bees. Fortunately, on that day, before Gershom went under for a third time, he had been rescued by Shmulik Fargessen who was fishing in the area. As a result of his fright and shock, and a morbid fear of being swept away into the Black Sea, and possibly into the mouth of a whale, he subsequently taught himself to swim. Mayor Chaim Kapoyer knew that Gershom had taught himself to swim. He also knew that residents were in danger of drowning because of their mistaken belief that because they had evolved from fish they must have inherited a natural ability to swim. He subsequently consulted Gershom regarding offering swimming lessons to the community, and Gershom agreed. Gershom was not the best swimmer, himself, but his rudimentary skills kept him from drowning whenever he was forced to run to the river in order to escape swarming bees.

Gershom subsequently posted a sign outside of his house which read "Nussbaum Honey and Swimming Lessons." Due to the resulting popularity of the swimming school, Mayor Chaim Kapoyer felt that his legacy had grown a bit more, and his father, the former Mayor Moishe Kapoyer, proudly realized that the little Town of Patchentuch was now in very capable hands.

The Liebeherz Legacy

Years ago when Melech Liebeherz, the scholar, wed Zlaate Perlmutter, the local Yentas predicted and really and truly hoped that he would now have less time to dedicate to his independent studies. Melech researched subjects such as gravity, evolution and other matters that appealed to his scientific curiosity, ideas that often caused anxiety in the remote shtetl town of Patchentuch, and in fact frightened many of its residents. Married or not, however, Melech continued his studies even more assiduously than before he was married, which was a disappointment to the Yentas and others. When their son, Nasich, admiring his father's intellect, followed in Melech's footsteps, he became a scholar just like his father.

Years later, when Nasich married Dvorah Plotsky, their son, Shlomo, also grew up to become a scholar who, like his father and grandfather, studied and did research on subjects that still made traditional Patchentuch residents uneasy and uncomfortable. When, years later, Shlomo married Raizel Frumkin, the seed of intellectual curiosity which had flourished in the Liebeherz family continued. The residents of the town closed their ears when informed of the latest Liebeherz research, the most recent having something to do with winged crafts that could fly, apparently defying the laws of gravity that Melech had talked about years earlier. In Patchentuch people no longer questioned the laws of gravity, (although they were not well understood) but they did occasionally look up at the sky to assure themselves that there was nothing up there that could possibly fall on them.

* * * * *

The old Yentas of the town had always believed that they knew

49

better than the shadchan about who was better suited to whom, and in the case of selecting wives for the Liebeherz men, it had been no different. In these cases the Yentas never gave up hope that, with the selection of *their* potential candidates for suitable wives, the creative ideas of the Liebehertz men might be diverted, and the people of Patchentuch would no longer have to listen to foolishness such as the idea that men were once monkeys. Fortunately in the interest of forward thinking and progress, the influence of the younger women, sometimes called Yentatas, had grown, and now overcame the wishes and intentions of the older and more traditional Yentas. These younger women, the Liebeherz wives, were, by the way, the women who religiously wore hand knit white shawls with blue stripes, but *without* fringes, to shul every Shabbos. Today, after all, belongs to the new generation, not to the old Yentas, and thank goodness for that.

Pinchas Reconsiders

Since Gimmel Lochinkopf emigrated to Palestine, Pinchas Plotz ran the bookstore by himself. Reluctantly, he relinquished his seat on the Mayor's Council because he now had little time to spare. Just before Gimmel left, however, he and Pinchas had considered the idea of possibly holding a series of informal lectures at the shop, so that people with a particular area of expertise might share their special knowledge. The shop could accommodate no more than a dozen people, but that seemed to be a reasonable number to justify an informal lecture series, and so Pinchas advertised it in his shop window. Those who were interested in offering a presentation were invited to sign up. It would be an educational and informative offering for a book shop, and so he prepared a sign announcing the upcoming lecture series, placed it in the window and waited for people to sign up.

Pinchas did not have to wait long before volunteers for speaking arrived and placed their names on the list. The first was Nasich Liebeherz who was prepared to present a lecture on men and monkeys. The next person to put his name on the list was Beymish Schmootz, the herbalist, who wished to give a talk on the benefits of weeds. Yitzhak Rozencrantz and Leybush Blum, the undertakers, wanted to discuss death and dying, whereas Yossel Plotz, a drayman and the brother of Pinchas, wanted to give a lecture on wagon wheels. Mendel Teitlebaum, a woodsman, wanted to talk about chopping down trees while Geshmak Feinkochen, the oculist, wanted to talk about going blind. When the women of the town heard about the proposed lecture series at the bookstore, they wondered why no women had signed up, and so Faigele Scheinkopf, the urgent care person of the town, decided to give a lecture on germs, whereas Fraidle Schmaltzberger wished to talk about chicken soup.

When he reviewed the list of volunteers Pinchas was not at all confident that the proposed subjects for lectures would attract much of an audience, and perhaps it would not be worth the bother. As far as a talk on the connection between men and monkeys, the subject was to be avoided at all cost. Evolution and religion, like oil and water, did not mix in the town of Patchentuch. Moreover, nobody wanted to hear about germs, which you couldn't see anyway, and certainly they did not want to be reminded of death and dying. The subject of wagon wheels sounded rather dull, (despite that Yossel was Pinchas's' younger brother,) and the topic concerning the chopping down of trees would be of interest to no one. Furthermore, the idea of disease might be off- putting, and as for chicken soup, all of Patchentuch knew as much about chicken soup as they cared or wanted to know.

Perhaps, thought Pinchas, a lecture series was not such a good idea, and if truth be told, after a hard day's work, who in Patchentuch would have the time or the interest in a lecture. Consequently, he abandoned the lecture series idea, but because he found he had been missing the "spirited" debates he experienced at Town Council meetings, he thought he might re-apply for membership.

A Panic In Patchentuch

One Shabbos afternoon following a Bar Mitzvah Schlamazel Lifshutz, the schnorrer, had just returned home from the celebration. He was content, albeit distressed from all the food he had eaten. The walk from the shul, along with the added weight of the food in his pockets, had worn him out, and so he sat down on his front stoop to catch his breath before climbing the three steps to his front door. Schlamazel breathed heavily and sighed, and he glanced up at the sky to thank God for the food he had received that day, both for the food he had eaten, as well as for the rest that was in his pockets. Schlamazel gazed up at the sky to thank his Lord when he noticed some moving objects above the clouds. His eyesight was failing, he knew, yet he could make out enough to see that they were not birds.

"Oy," though Schlamazel, "these are the flying objects that Melech and Nasich Liebeherz have been telling us about, and now they will fall to earth and crash and burn." Schlamazel immediately got up from the stoop where he was sitting. He had to sound the alarm, and so he hurried back to the shul where he found Mayor Chaim Kapoyer speaking with members of his flock. Schlamazel interrupted the conversation and excitedly related what he had witnessed in the sky that would soon be crashing to earth.

"Calm yourself, Schlamazel," the Mayor told him, "and speak slowly and explain."

"Melech has been right all along," he told the people, "and the flying objects he speaks of have arrived in Patchentuch. Look up and you will see." The Mayor, and the others who heard Schlamazel's panicked news, all looked up at the sky, and what they saw seemed to be only the remnants of what Schlamazel had seen, but see them, they did.

Whenever something out of the ordinary occurred in Patchentuch, something that could not be explained, the worst was always suspected. Melech had researched flying machines, and now that they were here people believed that they were in imminent danger.

As a consequence, women began to walk around the town with umbrellas over their heads, and with one eye on the sky, while men stuffed flat pieces of wood into the tops of their fur shtreimels, just in case. Residents regularly scanned the skies as panic spread. For days after the "sighting," the skies had been clear, and so there appeared to be no imminent danger, yet the residents of the town did not let down their guard. No one could predict when some machine would fly over Patchentuch, fall from the sky and crash and burn on top of their heads. Melech and his son Nasich were consulted, but they had not witnessed what Schlamazel had seen, and so they could not be sure. If it was a flying machine, they reassured, it was meant to fly and not to crash and burn. Science was not a danger, it was progress which should be embraced and not feared, but the residents of the town could not be persuaded.

For the entire following week all was quiet, and the people of the town went about their business, albeit with umbrellas over their heads and wood in their hats. The following Shabbos, however, their tranquility was again shattered when after services, flying objects were again sighted high up in the sky, and panic erupted once more. The objects seemed closer this time, and could be identified with the naked eye. What they turned out to be, however, were not unidentified flying machines after all, but simple kites on strings originating from the neighboring town of Schmertzburg. They had apparently broken away from the hands of children caused by the wind blowing toward Patchentuch. The relieved women of the town then put away their umbrellas, and the men removed the flat pieces of wood from inside their shtreimels, and life continued on, as it always had, in the little town of Patchentuch.

Where Is Yudel?

Farbisene Punim and Yudel Tzadrudelt were friends. When they met up in the street, now stooped over on a walking stick, they strolled slowly, sharing complaints about their physical ailments, of which each had many. Farbisene and Yudel lived solitary lives, except for when they met in the street and shared conversation, most of which neither could hear very well. When the weather permitted it was not unusual to see these two very old, and pretty much decrepit folks leaning on their walking sticks and talking as they strolled, both chatting at the same time. Neighbors sometimes helped them with food and shopping, but otherwise they were pretty much on their own.

One day Yudel decided not to get out of his bed in the morning. Why bother, he reasoned. What was there to get out of bed for? He could just as easily suffer his aches and pains in bed as when he was moving about, and so he spent the day in bed without going outside at all. Periodically he got up to prepare a cup of tea or eat a slice of bread, but otherwise he remained in bed and slept. The next day he did the same, and the day after that. When Farbisene did not see her friend in the street, and had not for several days, she became concerned. When she ran into Rebbe Benny she shared her concern regarding Yudel, and he suggested that she stroll over to his house and inquire after him, which she did.

Having never been inside his house she did not wish to intrude, but because she was genuinely worried, she overcame her reluctance. She slowly made her way, and when she arrived at his door she rapped with her walking stick. When there was no response she began to worry that her old friend, God forbid, might have died. She rapped again more forcefully, but still no response. As it turned out, Yudel had not died. He had just decided not to get out of bed. Why bother? When he eventually heard the loud raps on the door he rose from his bed, slowly making his way to the door where an agitated Farbisene stood.

"Oy, Farbisene," he said, "it is you."

"Of course it is me. Who else would it be? " a relieved Farbisene said. "So you are not dead," she told him.

"Why should I be dead?" he asked.

"And why not? You are old, I am old, and at any moment either one of us could drop dead. It wouldn't be such a surprise."

"No, I suppose not," Yudel told her, and they both laughed.

"So how are you?" she asked him.

"Not so good," he answered. "I am not yet dead, as you can see, but I know I am dying," he told her.

"Why do you think you are you dying?" she asked.

"Why not? Everyone dies sooner or later."

"Would some chicken soup help, do you think?"

"It might," he told her. "It certainly couldn't hurt," and so Farbisene returned home and cooked a pot of chicken soup for her friend.

* * * * *

Later that day, after consuming several bowls of the soup that Farbisene had prepared for him, Yudel began to feel better. He was not yet dying, after all; he just needed a reminder that someone cared, and Farbisene did, in her way. When she visited him the next time she brought with her another soup offering, this time with knaidles, and the two of them sat at his table and ate it together. Whenever he felt like he was dying she would bring him more. All he had to do was to ask.

Yudel Seeks an Apology

Farbisene Punim was almost the only person in Patchentuch who had really and truly befriended old Yudel Tzadrudelt, with the exception of Faigele Scheinkopf. When Faigele, the urgent care person of the town, occasionally stopped in to check on old Yudel, she might find Farbisene Punim there with her homemade chicken soup. Despite that Yudel continued to believe he might be dying, he still remained very much alive. Farbisene's chicken soup, especially with the added knaidles, had unquestionably helped.

One day when Faigele stopped by, Yudel was alone, and they sat down to talk.

"All is in God's hands," Faigele told him, "and you are not dying. You will live, and you will continue to walk and visit with Farbisene for many days to come, and you will continue to enjoy her chicken soup."

"Yes," Yudel told Faigele, "I will have her chicken soup, and I will not die. I will not die just yet," he repeated, "at least not until I get an apology from Rebbe Shalomovsky."

"Rebbe Shalomovsky?" Faigele asked. "You mean the old, retired Rebbe?"

"Yes, he is the one," replied a suddenly agitated Yudel. "He owes me an apology, and I cannot die until I receive it. The chicken soup will help to keep me alive until at least the time when he will apologize to me."

"For what does he owe you an apology?" Faigele asked.

"He insulted me, and he must apologize before I am willing to die, chicken soup or no chicken soup."

"How did he insult you?" inquired an incredulous Faigele.

"I can't remember," Yudel told her, "but I clearly remember that he did indeed insult me."

"If you cannot remember what he said or did to insult you, then how can you still be so upset?"

"I don't have to remember what he said or did in order to be upset," Yudel vehemently insisted.

"But, Yudel," replied Faigele, "Rebbe Shalomovsky is dead. He is no longer here to apologize."

"He is dead?"

"Yes, he is dead," Faigele repeated.

"Well, then," replied a surprised Yudel, "I will get up from my bed and eat the chicken soup that Farbisene has brought me. I suppose it makes no sense that I should lie here and wait for an apology that will never come."

And so Yudel Tzadrudelt rose from his bed, thanked Faigele, ate his chicken soup, dressed and put on a sweater. He then took his walking stick and went out into the street to look for Farbisene Punim, whom he hoped was also out for a stroll.

Zelig Is Confused

It was morning in the Schmaltzberger household, and Zelig was now dressed and ready for the day.

It was breakfast time, and Hetty, Zelig's wife, had set the table. She put out the bread and the pickled herring, and she called Zelig to come come and eat. She had heated a pot of water, poured it into the cups, added the tea, and put the regular two teaspoons of sugar into Zelig's cup. Her own cup sat on the counter next to his, but without sugar. When she carried the cups to the table, she could not exactly remember into which cup she had put Zelig's usual two teaspoons of sugar. Thinking that they might not be in the cup she had handed her husband, (which they were,) and she was confused as to which cup was actually his, to be on the safe side she added two more teaspoons of sugar to the cup she handed him. When Zelig took the first sip it was so sweet that he could not drink it.

"So now how will you fix it?" a disappointed Zelig asked. "I am already late for work."

"Not to worry, husband, I will fix it," and so she quickly removed the double sweetened cup of tea from the table, bringing it back to the counter. She then took a fresh cup from the cabinet into which she poured one half of the over sweetened tea from what she had thought was Zelig's cup, which it was, into the empty cup, adding to it a half a cup of hot water from the pot. When Hetty then returned to the kitchen table with Zelig's cup, she handed it to him. He took a sip, pronouncing it to be satisfactory, if not as strong as usual.

"So how did you fix it, Hetty?" he asked, and when she explained to her husband what she had done to fix the problem, Zelig, who was not one of the brightest of lights in the menorah, was totally confused. Nonetheless, he ate his bread and herring, and he drank his cup of tea, and Zelig thought what a clever wife he had.

Felix Comes To Patchentuch

One day Faigele Scheinkopf received a letter from Dr. Applebaum, her old mentor and medical colleague from Lodz. Over the years Faigele had learned a great deal from Dr. Applebaum about innovations in urgent care treatment. In his letter to Faigele he proposed to her that his son, Dr. Felix Applebaum, who was now a medical doctor, and who was also interested in philanthropy, wished to volunteer his medical services for two weeks in a small community such as Patchentuch. He wanted to share his medical knowledge, especially in the area of urgent care, about which he had recently learned. In an attempt to improve the condition of mankind, and being an idealist, he wished to share his newly acquired skills for the benefit of others. Dr. Applebaum wondered if Faigele would be willing to allow his son, the new doctor, to perform such a mitzvah, and, more importantly, could she use his help. Young Dr. Felix Applebaum would appreciate the experience of working with Faigele in her practice, and he would be happy to share his knowledge in urgent care treatment, his specialty.

* * * * *

Patchentuch was in the backwater of nowhere, so Dr. Felix from Lodz believed he could "revolutionize" urgent care medicine in the little town by virtue of the forward thinking medical research to which he had been exposed. He would share with Faigele all that he had learned, and in this way might change the face of Patchentuch urgent care. Shortly thereafter, young Dr. Felix arrived in Patchentuch, where, at Faigele's suggestion, he took a room in Hester Britchky's

Shtetl Betl. He brought his knowledge and enthusiasm, along with his medical bag, and was prepared to teach Faigele much that would help her in her practice.

On his very first day in the clinic he treated six patients. The first was Zlaate Fartumelt, the baker, who had burned her hand in the oven. The second patient was Betzalel Guta, the tallis maker who had run a needle through his finger. The third patient was Mendel Teitlebaum, the woodsman, who had grazed his hand with an axe. Perchik Schmaltzberger, the cobbler, had hammered his hand by mistake. Amos Farshimmelt, the rope maker, had rope burns on his hands, and Yossel Plotz, the drayman, had caught his foot under a wagon wheel. It appeared that Dr. Felix Applebaum had arrived just in time to lessen the work load of Faigele because the clinic was full.

After examining each of the six patients and cleansing their wounds and injuries, he gave them special salves and ointments that he had brought with him in his medical bag. He prescribed their daily use for a week, plus a frequent soaking of the wounds, as well as a return visit in a week.

On the next day there were several new patients, each complaining of headaches, irritation, swelling, and a variety of other aches and pains, and so Faigele was asked to take a look. For a learning experience, she took young Dr. Applebaum over to consult with Mendel Schmootz, the herbalist (and quasi pharmacist) who, after listening to all the complaints and symptoms, prescribed different medications for each one. For one he prescribed Beymish's Basil Blend; for another he prescribed Breindel's Basil Balm; for a third patient he prescribed Elderberry Compound, and for others he recommended Marvin's Bees Knees or Tateleh's Violet Blend and Sheldon's Bee Balm. Within a few days they all returned to tell Faigele and Felix of the rapid improvement in their various conditions.

* * * * *

Felix was astonished to learn that a local herbalist could provide plants and weeds that really worked quite well. Felix's two week commitment was soon up, and his period of service was over. In the end he had learned a great deal more from Faigele and Mendel Schmootz than they did from him. His salves and ointments had done no harm during his brief stay in the little town of Patchentuch, and neither had he, and on his return to Lodz, he had much to share with his colleagues about wildflowers and weeds.

Part Two

The Tallis

The young boys of Patchentuch studied under the tutelage of Rebbe Benny Rachmanes. During one of the most recent classes a student asked a question regarding the significance of the color blue in the tallis. Because it was near the end of the day and the boys were tired, Rebbe Benny decided to tell them a story regarding the Tallis and the color blue, and so he began.

The Story

In the late fifteenth century Spain life for the Jews had become intolerable. The evil of the Spanish Inquisition had reached a peak, and Jews who would not convert to Christianity were either forced to leave the country or be burned at the stake. At the time there lived in the city of Cordoba a weaver and a dyer, both devout Jews. Abraham Lopez was a weaver by trade and Benjamin Mendez, a dyer. They worked together to produce the prayer shawls for the once thriving Jewish community in Cordoba. Because of the dangers that now existed for the Jews of Spain the two families made the decision to leave the country, and after much agonizing and preparation they made their way across the Mediterranean Sea to a new life in Morocco. Sadly, the strain and stress of the journey adversely affected the two wives, and one died along the way, the other shortly after arrival. The two fathers, Abraham Lopez and Benjamin Mendez, both now young widowers, were left to care for their small children, Techela Lopez, a daughter, and a son, Joseph Mendez. Eventually the two fathers, along with their now motherless children, made their way to the town of Chefchaoen, once a Moorish fortress high in the Rif Mountains of Morocco. There the two fathers found a place to live, and together they opened a modest business. The children, Techela and Joseph were inseparable. Where one went the other followed.

Years passed, and life in Chefchaoen was good to both families.

More Jewish immigrants from Spain arrived, and eventually a substantial Jewish community established itself in this mountain town. It was a comfort to the Jews of Chefchaoen to live high up in the hills because it provided a feeling of closeness to God in heaven. They were a devout Jewish community, and they never forgot their religious obligations, praying twice daily, their heads covered by the holy tallis. Abraham was the weaver of these wool tallisim, and Benjamin, the dyer of the holy fringes. The problem was, and always had been, that the thread for the fringes prescribed by Jewish law, required blue dye, a sign of nobility, reminding the Jews that they were members of God's Kingdom of Priests. In order to obtain this particular color, the rare snail from the Mediterranean Sea that produced the dye must be found. Moreover, because the snails were difficult or nearly impossible to find, blue dye became a much sought after commodity. Only royalty was permitted the luxury of this dye, for kings were the only ones who could afford it. The dream of both fathers, Abraham and Benjamin, was to someday obtain the dye in order to produce the tallisim that strict Jewish law required.

Techela and Joseph grew up in homes with fathers who dreamed of blue dye and the rare snails that produced it. It was the music that had accompanied their daily lives in Cordoba and in the Rif Mountains of Morroco. Techela, herself, dreamed of the sought after color, the shade of her own blazing sapphire eyes. Years later when Techela married Joseph, they made a secret pact to embark on a search for the illusive snails for the fathers who had sacrificed so much in order to give them a life.

Months after Joseph and Techela were married they decided to put their plan for discovering the rare snails into action. Had they been younger the fathers, themselves, might have undertaken the search, but their time had long passed. Moreover, had they known of their children's secret plan, they would have discouraged it. The journey through the vast and rocky Rif Mountains was arduous and dangerous, and the threat of wild animals and bandits was ever present. When, and if, they reached the seacoast, the ocean could be treacherous, and diving for the snails would present a grave threat.

The fathers would never sanction such a journey on the part of their beloved children, and Joseph and Techela knew this. It is for that reason they kept their intentions secret from Abraham and Benjamin, and they made their plans secretly.

Techela, who had learned the art of weaving from her father Abraham, spent her spare time weaving the net in which she would carry back the snails for her father and father in law. Carefully she sewed amulets against the evil eye into the woven fabric, and with each step her impatience grew. The time for their departure approached, and with every passing day she and Joseph became more anxious. At night in the privacy of their room they discussed plans and provisions for the journey. They knew that the Rif Mountains were forbidding; the steep granite cliffs were especially dangerous, and sudden deep valleys and gorges presented peril to anyone with the temerity to venture into the mountains. Neither Joseph nor Techela was an experienced climber, and although they had lived in the mountains most of their lives, they were respectful of the hazards presented by the towering giants surrounding them. Both, however, preferred to think of the challenges in positive terms. In their dreams they conjured up jeweled green valleys and cliff walls aglow with orange and red shafts of sunlight. They dreamed of gentle mountain streams and picturesque peaks, lush green forests and nights together spent under the stars and cloudless skies. Slippery ledges and rockslides were not part of their dreams, only magical lagoons in which they would refresh themselves. An occasional goat would come into view, and they would laugh together, enjoying the sight. They would be Adam and Eve in the Garden of Eden, surrounded by slopes covered with flowering herbs. In their dreams there were no perilous rapids, only incredible lush cedar forests primeval. Along the journey they would rest and enjoy picnics of goat cheese, couscous and bread. They would drink water from natural mountain streams, and they would sleep under the stars. Their dreams were ethereal, and at the end of the rainbow they would discover the snails, which they would carry back to their beloved fathers.

Joseph and Techela expected that nights in the hills would be cold and the days hot. What they never imagined was how bitterly cold and how blistering hot they would be, a reality they would soon discover. Before sunrise on the day of their departure they left a note for their sleeping fathers informing them of their plans, reassuring them that God would watch over them. They then silently slipped away into the darkness. Techela had filled her woven net with provisions they would need, a net she held close to her body at all times. With God's help they would make the return trip with a net filled with the precious snails.

When the sun rose over the Rif Mountains they were well on their way. During all the years they had lived in Chefchaoun they had developed an innate sense of the direction to the Mediterranean Sea. From casual conversations with village elders, they knew about the town of Bou-Ahmed and were confident that within a week's time they could make the trip to this town which was a direct route from Chefchaoun to the sea. Never having been to the coast, except for when they were young children and had emigrated from Spain, they were excited at the prospect of casting their eyes upon the seashore. In their imagination they conjured up romantic visions of a town with bazaars filled with spices, carpets and jewels. They imagined that any place outside of Chefchaoun was redolent of mystery. Perhaps there would be sultans' palaces, elaborate mosaic covered mosques and minarets, and things similar in flavor to Chefchaoun, but on a grander scale. First, however, they would have to navigate the mountains with their unknown risks and dangers.

The day was bright and sunny, and at mid morning they stopped for something to eat. Joseph was quiet when Techela asked him what he was thinking. Joseph looked up at his young wife.

"Do you think we have made a mistake? Is this a foolish thing we have undertaken? By agreeing to make this journey have I endangered you?" and he lowered his head into his hands.

"No, my dear," Techela told him. "By agreeing to this adventure you have given me what I have longed for. God bless you, and let us talk of this no more." With her words Joseph was comforted, and they continued together on their way. The route turned treacherous, and was steeper than they had anticipated, with rockslides and scorpions a constant concern. They encountered gorges in high places, and risked slipping off of steep granite cliffs. Level places to spend nights were hard to find, and by the fourth morning they were exhausted and bruised by their perilous descent.

In their dreams the young couple believed it was possible to navigate the mountains but the reality proved otherwise. All paths began to look the same, and often times they were not sure if they had retraced their steps and traveled in circles. They became discouraged when their daily treks appeared to take them no closer to the sea. There were times when Techela stumbled, bruising her body or twisting an ankle and could walk no further.

"Am I am holding us back, Joseph?" she pleaded, tears in her eyes.

"You are not holding us back," he told her. "We are in this together, and we will do the best we can, together," and he gently wiped away the tears, allowing her to rest in a forest glen.

Food was running low, so Techela and Joseph had taken to eating berries from the trees and bushes that grew wild in the forest. When they came upon a mountain stream they drank and refreshed their weary bodies, but it was not the euphoria they had dreamed of. The nights were frigid, and Techela was alarmed by the ghostly howling of unseen animals. She hoped and prayed that the light of their campfire would keep them safe. They were never certain of where they were going or if they were getting any closer to the ocean, and then one morning the air suddenly began to feel and smell different. Perhaps, after all, they had descended to a lower altitude without realizing it. They could only hope, and so they pushed on. Techela worried about their old fathers for she understood the distress and extreme worry they must be enduring.

Suddenly one morning they were jolted from their sleep by the music of tinkling bells, and when they discovered the source of the sound they were encouraged to spot a distant herd of goats with a goatherd near by. Approaching the young man, they inquired about the route to Bou- Ahmed and the coast.

"Look there," he told them pointing East. "See the haze yonder?

When the sun climbs higher in the sky the haze will disappear and you will sea the sea. Bou- Ahmed is there," and so with renewed vigor they pressed on. They did not stop until they reached the sea. That night the two exhausted lovers camped on a rocky shore listening to the roar of the surf as it rolled in and onto the beach. In their excitement they could hardly wait until morning in order to begin their search. They fell asleep in one another's arms dreaming of the snails they would find and bring back to their fathers.

When Joseph and Tachela awoke in the morning, however, the weather was not what they had expected. Their sleep had been so sound that they never felt the change that had come during the early hours of the morning. The skies were gray and overcast, and the winds were whipping around with uncharacteristic force. It was not what they had expected, because during most of their mountain trek the weather had been hot and dry. This was not a day to dive for snails, a fact made eminently clear by an angry churning sea. Techela began to cry.

"Oh, Joseph," she sobbed, "how can this be? We have come so far, and now this." He took his wife in his arms and comforted her. "Perhaps it is as good thing," he told her. "It is better we should have a day of rest. We are tired and will need all of our endurance for the snails. Tomorrow, or the next, will be better." Tomorrow, however was not better, and a demoralized Techela was inconsolable. One could not dive in wind and choppy seas. As young children in Cordoba both had learned to swim, but they were not so experienced and confident that they could risk an angry ocean. They would have to wait until the waters becalmed.

They spent the days roaming the city, using coins they had carried with them for food, and passing the time in nervous anticipation of their underwater expedition. Moreover they were anxious to return to their fathers who would surely be sick with worry. They would most probably be expecting the worst, imagining that their children had been set upon by brigands or attacked by wild animals, or worse.

On the third day after their arrival the weather changed. When they awoke in the morning they were greeted by the sun. There was still a breeze in the air, but nothing like what they had experienced before. It appeared to be a day that favored a first attempt at seeking out the snails. Techela was ready with her net, but Joseph was not convinced that the waters had quieted enough to ensure a safe dive.

"Perhaps we should wait one more day," he told Techela. "The currents may still be strong, and we could be swept away. You never can know what it might be like under the water after a system such as this passes." Techela, however, was impatient.

"It will be fine," she told him. "The sun is out and the weather is good," but Joseph was not convinced.

"The currents could be still agitated beneath the surface, and the bottom silt has been so disturbed as to have made it difficult to even see snails, or anything else for that matter."

"Please," she begged. "If it is not good we will turn back, but at least we may see and judge with our own eyes. We cannot wait much longer," and so Joseph reluctantly agreed, but on the condition that if conditions did not favor a safe drive they would immediately end their search for the day.

They would first test the waters and their elementary diving skills, and would cautiously acclimate themselves before attempting to search for the snails. Neither had been swimming in the ocean for some time, and so, tentatively, they began. When they went under the water it was not as clear as they had hoped. The storminess of the past days had agitated the silt and sand on the ocean floor, as Joseph had suspected, and they could not see clearly. When they dove beneath the surface they became disoriented and needed to restore their bearings. The water was warm, soothing their aching bodies, the salt cleansing their wounds. The sea air was a balm to their pain, and they swam before seriously undertaking their search. What if the journey had been a fool's errand? Moreover, they weren't even certain they knew what these snails looked like. They had been told that they had striped shells, but that is all they knew. Would that be enough to identify them? Had they been foolish and impetuous to think they might ever discover what they sought? Had they been seduced by a pipe dream?

Several more days passed before they felt comfortable in the ocean waters which were reluctantly calming down. They had become more skillful at holding their breath before diving into the ocean's depths, and every hour emboldened them. Anyone who saw them in the water might have mistaken them for two dolphins at play. Each hour they pressed themselves to swim farther and deeper. The visibility had improved, allowing them to observe sea life at the bottom. Just as they were preparing to end their search for the day something drew Techela's attention. She was tired, and the daylight was beginning to fade. Cool breezes had blown in from the far horizon, and a squall was threatening, but her eye was drawn to a shape and form she could not resist. She beckoned to Joseph who was near by, and she readied the woven net that hung from her body. Hearing her call he followed, and down they both dove to investigate.

Back in the town of Chefchaoun a mantle of worry and concern lay heavily upon Abraham Lopez and Benjamin Mendez. The young people, now gone for weeks, had disappeared from their lives, and there was no way to learn of their fate. The fathers feared the worst. They had heard tales about those who became disoriented and were lost forever in the unforgiving Rif Mountains. They found it incredulous that their beloved children had imagined they were up to the task, their children who had lived in the mountains but never experienced their hazards. For all they knew, Techela and Joseph could have been attacked by wolves or outlaws or they could have slipped off a cliff somewhere into no-man's-land, never to be found. A whole range of frightening possibilities crossed their minds, and the fathers were sick with worry and grief, but what could they do?

When the Jews of Chefchaoun learned of the family's plight, one after another volunteered to undertake a search. A man called Ezra, who knew the most direct route to the sea, offered to lead a search. Unlike the perilous journey undertaken by Techela and Joseph, this trip took half as long, and when they reached the seacoast they asked questions. They traveled the length and breadth of the coast searching for information regarding the whereabouts of the young couple. They walked and they searched and they inquired, but learned nothing. When Ezra and his group finally arrived in the coastal town of Bou-Ahmed they continued to asked their questions, and it was here, at last, that they received answers.

Yes, people had seen the young couple, the ones who slept on the beach at night and were in the water all day. The woman had carried a net with her. Yes, they had seen them, and then they had not. One day they were here, and then they were gone. It appeared that they had disappeared soon after a storm, when the ocean was trying to make peace with the winds and currents. Yes, they were seen off the coast of Bou-Ahmed, and they had been inquiring about snails with striped shells. The Jews from Chefchaoun were encouraged to hear the news, but disturbed by the fact of their sudden disappearance. Where were they? Were they still in the area of Bou-Ahmed and more importantly were they still alive? It was becoming more apparent to Ezra and his group that the outcome might not be what they had hoped and prayed for. Nevertheless, they pressed on, searching for clues. When they had almost given up any hope of finding the couple, they came across a stone embankment along the rocky shore. The arrangement of the stones was such that a small pool of water collected along the shore, partly enclosed by rocks. Within the pool, a cave like structure had been created, and Ezra sighted what appeared to be a woven net lying within the aperture. Upon closer scrutiny the net appeared to be dotted with amulets, the kind often found in Chefchaoun. He bent over and lifted the net from the water. Inside was a collection of striped snails, snails that were alive because they had remained submerged in the salty ocean. Could it be? Could this be Techela's net with the rare snails they were seeking? If so, where were Techela and Joseph? Ezra shuddered to think.

* * * * *

Sadly, Techela and Joseph Lopez were never found, and it was assumed that the ocean had taken the young couple. Abraham Lopez and Benjamin Lopez died shortly after receiving the news. It was more than their gentle hearts could bear. Before their deaths, however, during the period of mourning for their lost children, they were able to extract blue dye from the snails that Ezra and his party had brought back from the sea. They were the able to fashion two holy tallisim from the gift that their beloved children had bestowed. Both fathers were buried in these tallisim, wrapped in the loving arms of their children who had sacrificed so much for the fathers they loved.

After their deaths the Jews of Chefchaoun diluted what was left of the blue dye, which was called Techelet, and with it they painted the home of the Lopez/Mendez family as a memorial to the love and devotion of the families.

As years passed and blue paint became available, house after house in the town of Chefchaoun was painted blue in tribute to the Lopez/Mendez family, until the entire town was swathed in the mystical color of the heavens. Today, if one visits the place in the Rif Mountains of Morocco, the town is still there, so many centuries later. Like a beautiful sapphire it sparkles under the golden sun, and the spirit of Joseph and Techela Lopez hovers over its rooftops like a blessing.

Printed in the United States
by Baker & Taylor Publisher Services